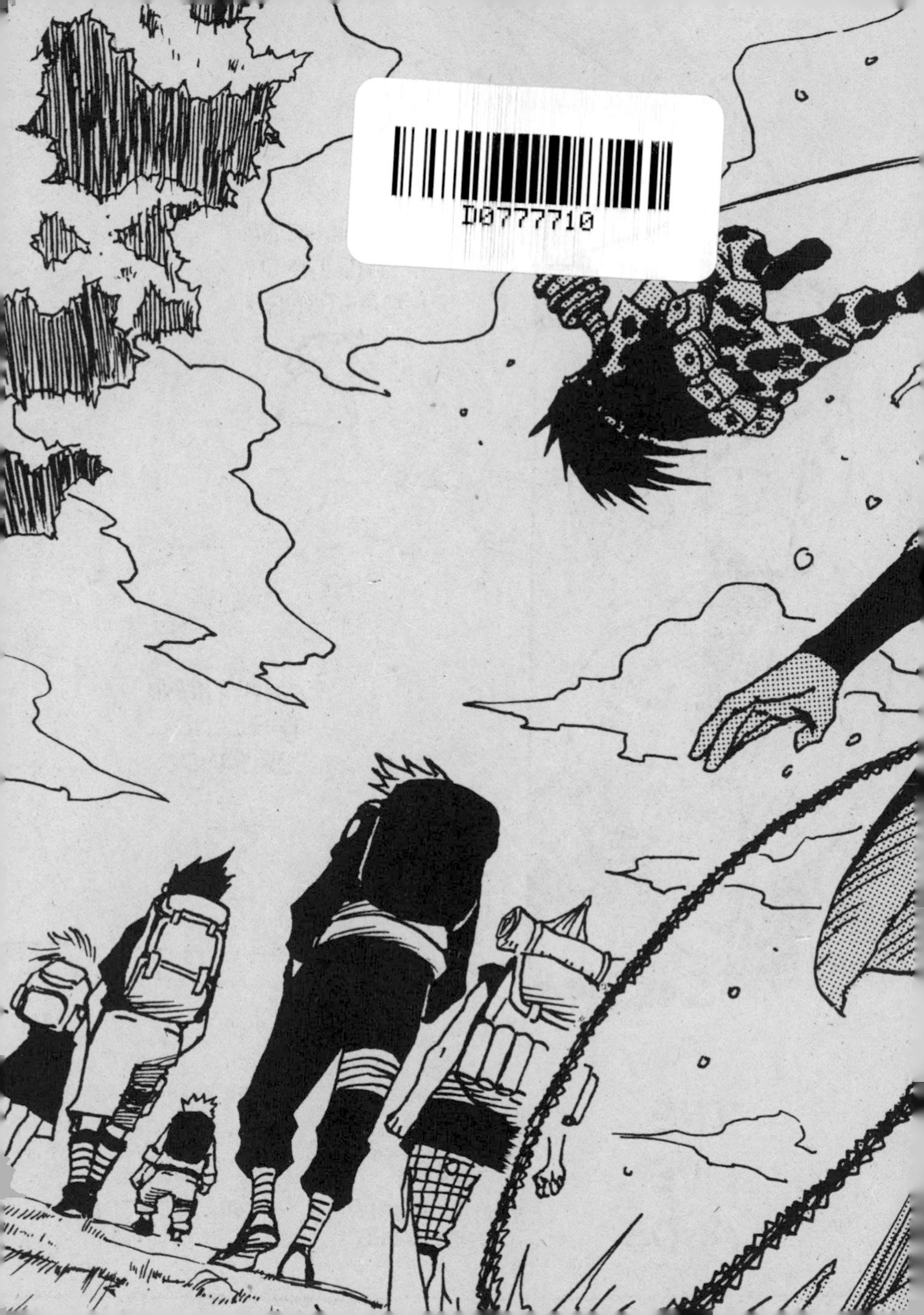

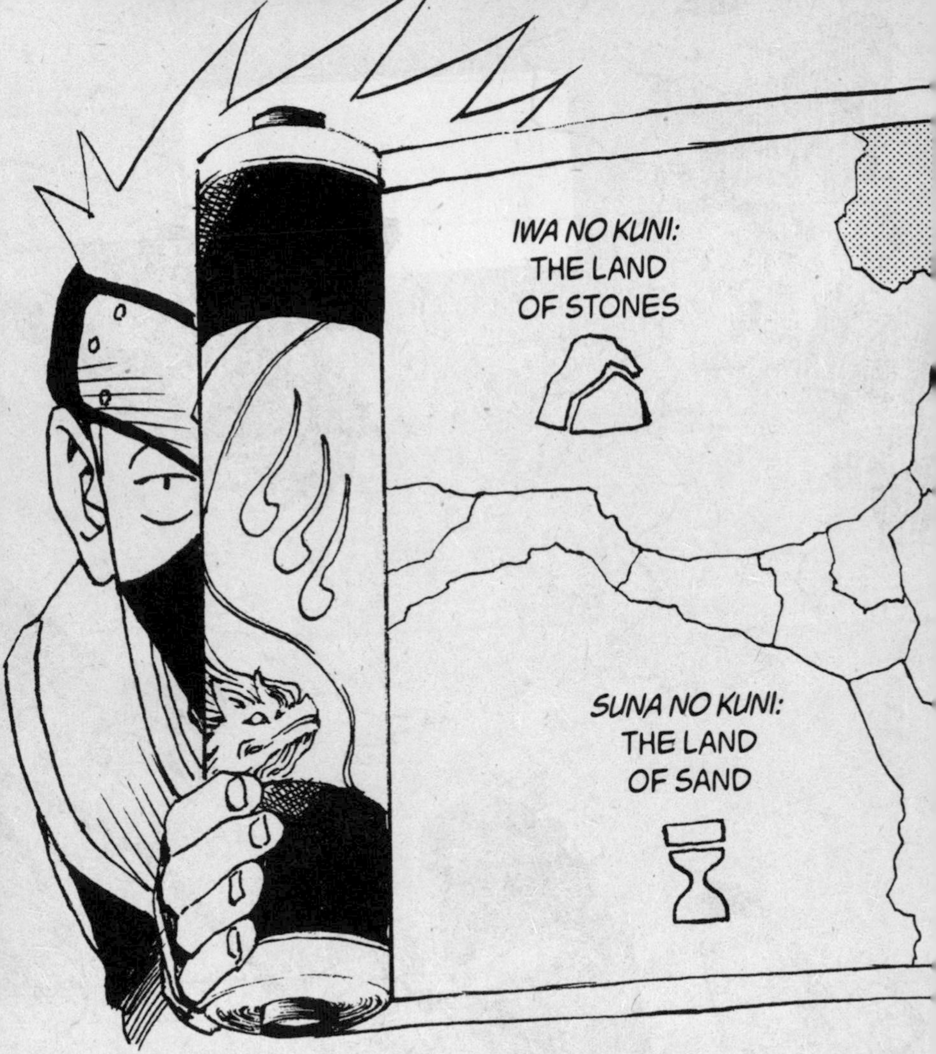
IWA NO KUNI:
THE LAND
OF STONES
SUNA NO KUNI:
THE LAND
OF SAND

THE FIVE LANDS

THE FIRE SHADOW

KONOHA NO KUNI KONOHAGAKURE NO SATO:

VILLAGE HIDDEN IN THE LEAVES

THE WATER SHADOW

KIRO NO KUNI KIRIGAKURE NO SATO:

VILLAGE HIDDEN IN THE MIST

KUMO NO KUNI:
THE LAND OF
THE CLOUDS

KIRO NO KUNI:
THE LAND OF
MIST AND FOG

KONOHA NO KUNI:
THE LAND OF
TREE AND LEAF

THE LIGHTNING SHADOW

KUMO NO KUNI
KUMOGAKURE
NO SATO:

**VILLAGE HIDDEN
IN THE CLOUDS**

THE WIND SHADOW

SUNA NO KUNI
SUNAGAKURE
NO SATO:

**VILLAGE HIDDEN
IN THE SAND**

THE EARTH SHADOW

IWA NO KUNI
IWAGAKURE
NO SATO:

**VILLAGE HIDDEN
IN THE SHADOW**

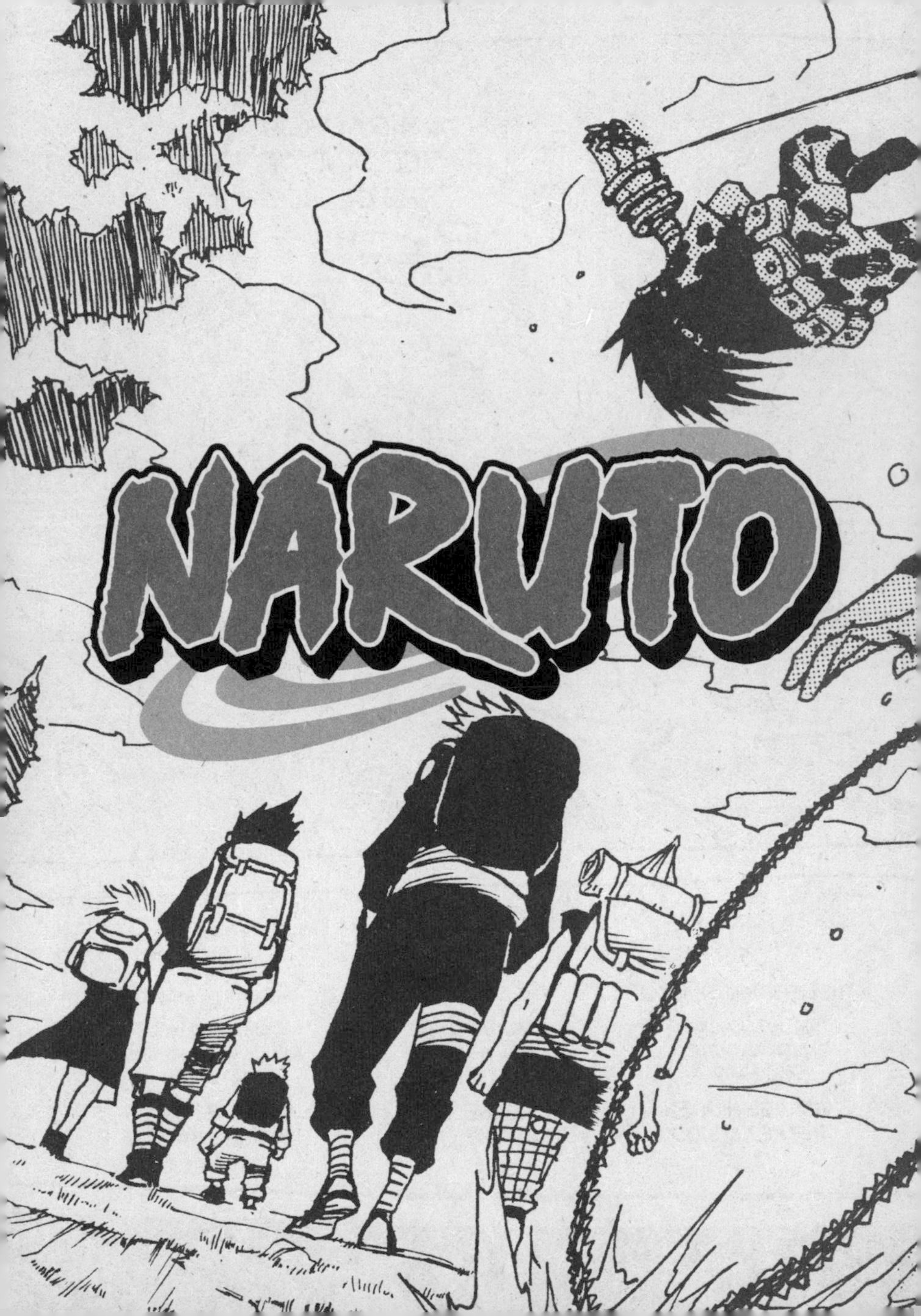
NARUTO

THE WORST JOB

ORIGINAL STORY BY **MASASHI KISHIMOTO**

ADAPTED BY TRACEY WEST

vizkids

VIZ MEDIA
SAN FRANCISCO

NARUTO THE WORST JOB
CHAPTER BOOK 3

Illustrations: Masashi Kishimoto
Design: Courtney Utt

Published by VIZ Media, LLC
P.O. Box 77010
San Francisco, CA 94107

www.viz.com

West, Tracey, 1965-
 The worst job / original story by Masashi Kishimoto ; adapted by
Tracey West ; [illustrations, Masashi Kishimoto].
    p. cm. -- (Naruto ; 3)
 Summary: Ninja-in-training Naruto must abandon his jokester ways when he
receives his first assignment to protect a famous bridge builder.
 ISBN 1-4215-2214-4
 [1. Ninja--Fiction. 2. Japan--Fiction.] I. Kishimoto, Masashi, 1974- II. Title. PZ7.W51937Wo 2008
 [Fic]--dc22
                            2008020189

Printed in the U.S.A.
First printing, November 2008
Second printing, December 2018

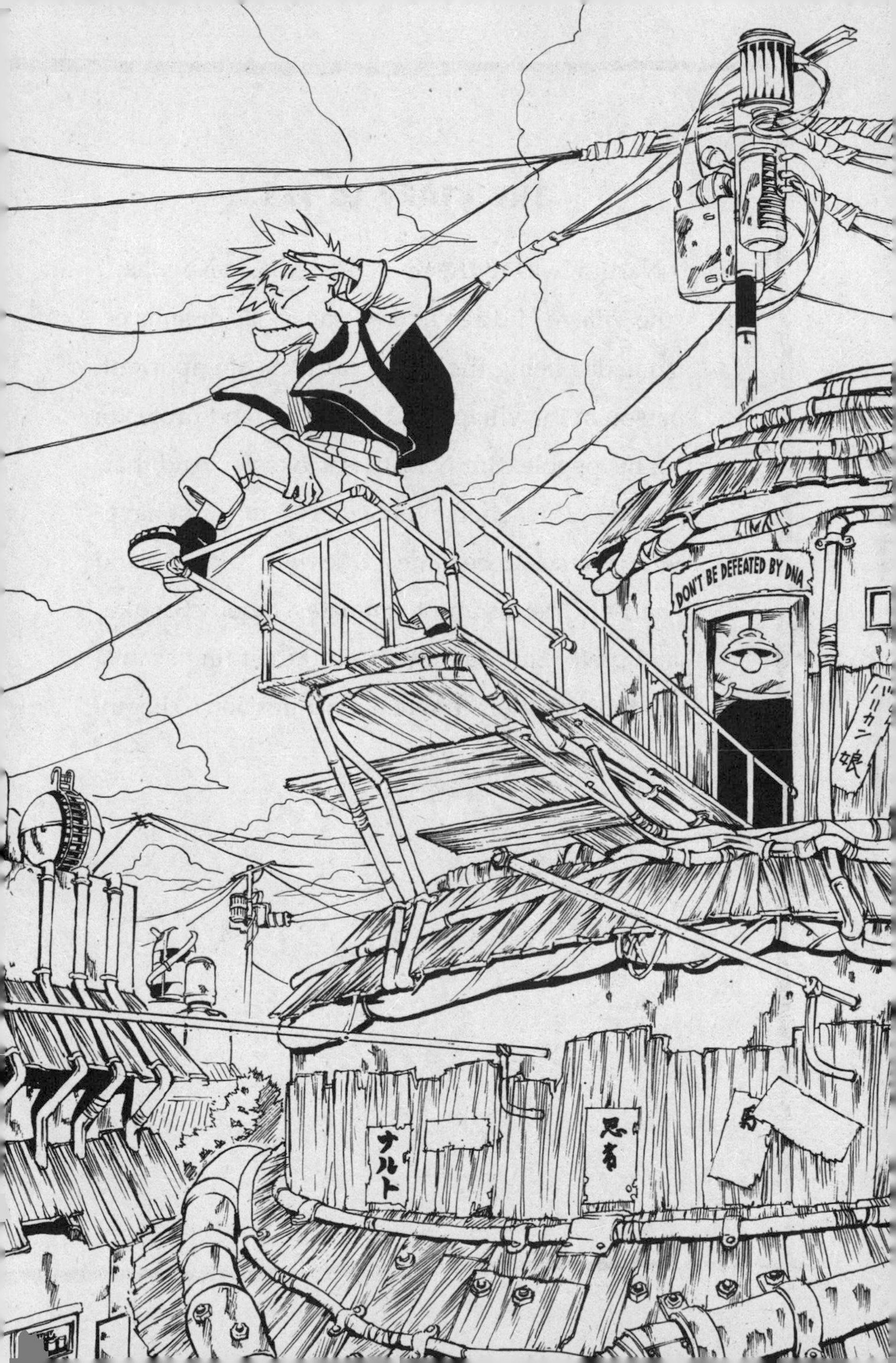
DON'T BE DEFEATED BY DNA
バリカン娘
ナルト
忍者

THE STORY SO FAR...

Naruto lives in the ninja universe, in Konoha, the Village Hidden in the Leaves. He dreams of someday being the Hokage, the most important person in the village and the leader and protector of his people. But Naruto is a jokester. And that makes his teachers worry that he may not have what it takes to become a true ninja. Now he and his new friends and teammates, moody Sasuke and pretty Sakura, have passed their first exams. It's time for their first real ninja mission to begin!

Naruto
ナルト

Naruto is training to be a ninja. He's a bit of a clown. But deep down, he's serious about becoming the world's greatest ninja!

Sakura
春野サクラ

Naruto and Sasuke's classmate. She has a crush on Sasuke, who ignores her. In return, she picks on Naruto, who has a crush on *her*.

Sasuke
うちはサスケ

The top student in Naruto's class and a member of the prestigious Uchiha clan.

1

LORD HOKAGE sat at a long table with a stack of papers. The leader of the Leaf Village stroked his white beard as he made his decision. Some of the top ninja in the village sat at the table with him.

The members of Squad Seven watched him anxiously. The three young ninja waited to hear what their next assignment would be. Sasuke, a black-haired boy in a dark blue shirt, stood calmly, without moving. A girl named Sakura pushed aside a strand of her pale pink hair to look at Sasuke. And Naruto, a short boy with spiky blond hair, impatiently tapped his foot.

Behind them stood Kakashi, their sensei. The teacher's hands were stuffed into the pockets of his black pants. He wore a green vest, and a black mask covered the bottom half of his face. Like the other ninja, he wore a headband with a metal plate on the front. The symbol of the Leaf Village was carved into the metal. Kakashi always wore his headband over his left eye.

"Let's see," said Lord Hokage. "The next assignment for Squad Seven will be…hmmm …babysitting? Running errands? Ah, here's one: the farmers need help digging sweet potatoes."

"NO WAY!" Naruto exploded. "Those jobs

are so boring! Give us something important to do! Something amazing!"

Naruto's fellow squad members were still getting used to his personality.

Secretly, Sasuke was glad Naruto had spoken up. He didn't want to dig potatoes either.

Sakura was embarrassed. Naruto could be such a pain!

Kakashi held back a sigh. Naruto had barely graduated from Ninja Academy. He was lucky to be a junior ninja now.

Master Iruka had taught Naruto at the academy. He sat next to Lord Hokage, helping to give out the squad assignments. Now he stood up, angry.

"Naruto, don't be a fool!" he shouted.

"You're only a beginner. Everyone starts out doing boring jobs. It's how you get experience. Then you can work your way up to bigger things."

Naruto stomped his foot. They had spent weeks doing stupid things like finding lost cats and cleaning floors. He was sick of it.

"We've done tons of small stuff. Can't we get some action?" he asked.

Kakashi bopped Naruto on the head. **"KNOCK IT OFF, NARUTO!** That's enough!"

Lord Hokage was a bit more patient. "Maybe I should explain things to Naruto," he said. "You see, every day our village receives many requests. The request could be as simple as babysitting, or as difficult as fighting off a ninja army. We sort the requests into categories from A to D. An A request is very difficult, and a D request is very easy."

Naruto held back a yawn.

The Hokage went on. "Then we divide the ninja into classes, based on their skills. The Hokage is the leader. Then come the jonin, the senior ninja, like your sensei, Kakashi. The next class is chunin, or journeyman ninja. Master Iruka is a chunin. The junior ninja are called genin—that's what you are, Naruto. And when you were in Ninja Academy, you were a cadet."

Naruto nodded. He knew all that stuff already.

"Then I sort through the requests," Lord Hokage explained. "The A-level tasks go to the jonin. Chunin get B- and C-level tasks.

And the genin, like you, get D- or sometimes C-level tasks. If the ninja completes the task, the grateful person he has helped pays him a fee."

Lord Hokage pointed to Squad Seven. "You three are low-level genin," he said. "Level D tasks are all you can hope to do."

Naruto wasn't even listening anymore. He sat on the floor, daydreaming about his next meal.

"Yesterday I had pork ramen noodles for lunch, so today I'll have miso ramen..."

"Are you even listening?" Master Iruka yelled.

Naruto folded his arms across his chest. "I don't want to hear it! All the old fart ever does is apologize and then give me a lecture!"

Kakashi groaned quietly. "I'm sorry," he told Lord Hokage. As a teacher, Naruto's bad behavior was his responsibility.

Naruto was shouting now. "But it's not fair! There's more to me than the trouble-making loser the old man thinks I am!"

Kakashi sighed. *I am going to be in so much trouble for this later…*

Master Iruka looked stunned by Naruto's outburst. Lord Hokage said nothing for a moment. Finally, he spoke.

"Very well," he said calmly.

"What?" Naruto was expecting to get yelled at. Sasuke and Sakura looked shocked. Even Kakashi was surprised.

"Since you put it that way, I'll give you a **C-level** task," Lord Hokage said. *The only way the boy can express himself is through pranks*, the leader reasoned. *Maybe giving him a real task to do will keep him out of trouble.*

"All right!" Naruto cheered.

"Squad Seven will be protecting a traveler," Lord Hokage told them.

Naruto jumped to his feet. "Who is it? Some great lord? A princess?"

"Calm down," Lord Hokage told him. "I will introduce you right now."

The Hokage nodded to a ninja by the door. "Please invite him in."

The ninja opened the door, and an old man stepped in. His gray hair and beard were messy. His clothes were old and faded. He frowned when he saw Squad Seven.

"Is this a joke?" he asked. "These kids can't be ninja. They look like a bunch of brats. Especially the short one. He looks like he hasn't got a brain."

Naruto laughed at first. "Ha! That's funny. No brain. . ."

He looked at Sasuke and Sakura. Then he realized he was the short one.

"Hey!" Naruto cried.

The man shrugged and glared at Lord Hokage. "I can't believe you're sticking me with such a sorry-looking squad!"

SCROLLS: (1) EARTH STYLE (2) FIRE STYLE (3) WATER STYLE (4) WIND STYLE (5) KISHIMOTO TECHNIQUE (6) NINJA WEAPONRY (7) NINJA CENTERFOLD (8) SUMMONING

"**LET ME AT HIM!**" Naruto screamed.

Kakashi held Naruto back by his jacket collar. "Naruto, you can't beat up the man you're supposed to protect."

"I am Tazuna, a famous bridge builder," the old man said. "I am going back to my country to finish a bridge I am working on. You all will have to protect me on the way— even if it costs you your lives!"

Naruto gave the floor a kick but kept quiet.

Everyone rushed home and quickly got

ready for the trip. First they packed food and water into their backpacks. Then they headed to the tall gates that protected the village.

Naruto looked through the open gates. The wide road stretched out in front of them. He pumped his arms in the air.

"ROAD TRIP!" he shouted happily.

"What are you so excited about?" Sakura asked.

"This is the first time in my life I've been outside the village!" Naruto replied. He did a happy dance, shaking his hips.

Tazuna scowled. "Am I really expected to place my life in the hands of this fool?"

"There's no reason to worry," Kakashi told him. "I am a jonin, and I'll be with you the whole way too."

"Listen, you old geezer, you don't mess with ninja, ever!" Naruto yelled. "Especially a good one like me. One day, I'm going to be the next Lord Hokage. So remember my

IT'S UZUMAKI NARUTO.

I AM THE CREAM OF THE ELITE. IN FACT, ONE DAY I'M GONNA BE THE NEXT LORD HOKAGE! SO REMEMBER MY NAME.

name—Naruto Uzumaki!"

"You want to be the Hokage, the leader of your village?" Tazuna laughed. "Give me a break!"

"You'd better watch out, mister," Naruto shot back. "When I'm Lord Hokage, you're going to have to show me a lot more respect!"

"Respect you? I don't think so," Tazuna replied. "Not even if you do become Hokage."

Naruto raised his hands, ready to attack. "That's it! You are going down!"

Kakashi pulled him back. "I said no hurting the client, you little **DUNCE,**" he scolded.

They marched down the road. The sun shone brightly overhead. Tall trees on either side of the road gave them some shade. For a while, the only noise was the sound of feet crunching in the dirt. Then Sakura spoke.

"Mr. Tazuna, you're from the Land of Waves, right?" she asked.

"What of it?" the old man replied grumpily.

Sakura looked at Kakashi. "Sensei, are there ninja in that land too?"

"No, not in the Land of Waves," Kakashi told her. "But that's unusual. Most other lands have their own hidden villages where a ninja clan resides. The ninja act as each land's military force. A small island, like the Land of Waves, is protected by the water around it. So it doesn't need a ninja force."

Kakashi took a scroll from his backpack.

He unrolled it. It showed a map of the continent. The five major lands were labeled.

"Each ninja village is hidden inside the land," the teacher explained. He pointed to the map. "There is the Leaf Village, where we live. Other hidden villages are the Mist Village, the Sand Village, the Stone Village, and the Cloud Village."

Naruto gazed at the map. The Leaf Village was located in what was once called the Land of Tree and Leaf, now known as the Land of Fire. This country was bordered by land on the west and water on the east. They must be headed toward the water.

"The Kage who rule each village are known as the five shadows," Kakashi went on. "They command thousands of ninja all over the world."

"Really? Lord Hokage is so amazing!" Sakura gushed. But that wasn't what she was thinking. *That boring old guy is famous? I can't believe it!*

"I know," Kakashi said, as though he read her mind. "None of you can believe that our Hokage is so powerful. Don't worry, I won't tell him.

"Anyway, sometimes the ninja of each land war against each other," Kakashi went on. "But we don't have to worry about that on this trip. This is a level C job. We might just have to deal with a stray robber or two."

"So we won't have to fight any foreign ninja?" Sakura asked. She was still a little worried.

Kakashi gave her a pat on the head. "Ha! Of course not."

They walked on. A small puddle lay in the path up ahead, and they walked around it. Kakashi glanced at it as they passed. A few steps later, Sakura let out a loud cry.

"Sensei!" Sasuke yelled.

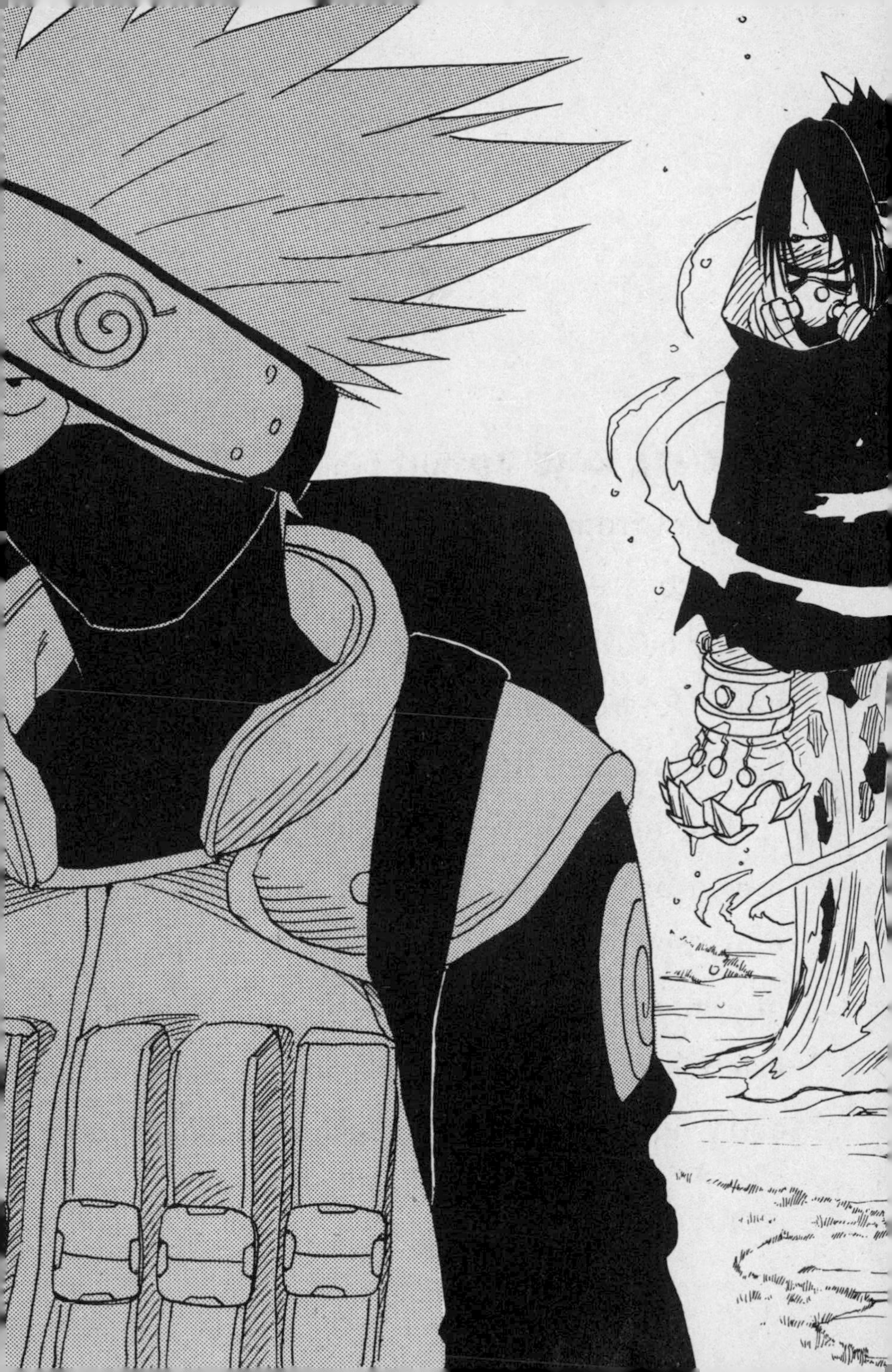

A NINJA ROSE UP out of the puddle. Water dripped from his black cloak. A metal gas mask covered the lower half of his face, and a gray headband held back his shaggy black hair. He wore metal gloves that made his hands look like sinister claws.

The ninja flew out of the puddle, followed by another, identical ninja. The two ninja brothers moved like the wind, jumping on either side of Kakashi. Each brother extended a spiked chain from his wrist armor and whipped it around Kakashi. He collapsed to the ground as the chains struck. The two brothers then jumped into the trees.

"Master Kakashi!" Naruto cried.

It had all happened so fast. Naruto, Sasuke, and Sakura were stunned. They didn't know what to do.

The dark ninja jumped out of the trees and

landed on either side of Naruto.

"You're *next*," one whispered.

Naruto felt a sharp stab of pain as one of the ninja's metal claws grazed the top of his left hand. A shockwave of fear tore through

Naruto's body. He was too scared to move. Each ninja brother flicked a spiked chain whip in the air, ready to attack.

Sasuke sprang into action. He launched himself into the air, reaching for his holster. He expertly threw a sharp shuriken at one of the chains. The throwing star caught the chain and pierced a nearby tree trunk, pinning the chain and the ninja to the tree.

The ninja turned and glared at Sasuke, fury in his eyes. With perfect aim, Sasuke quickly hurled a kunai at the other ninja's chain. Both brothers were now pinned to the same tree.

Sasuke didn't wait for the brothers to break free. He leapt up and landed on them, planting his feet on their claw arms.

WHAP! They cried out in pain as Sasuke grabbed each brother's head and slammed them together.

Fueled by anger, the ninja broke the chains, freeing their wrists. Sasuke went flying backward.

The ninja split up, one rushing toward Naruto, the other aimed right for Tazuna.

Sakura's heart pounded with fear. She'd seen the ninja take down Kakashi with her own eyes. But this was no time to be ruled by fear.

A fierce look filled her eyes. She jumped

in front of Tazuna, putting herself in the ninja's path.

"Stand back!" she cried out to the bridge builder.

She held her kunai in front of her, ready to use it. The ninja raised his armored claw hand.

Sasuke jumped to his feet. Their mission was to protect the old man. He jumped in front of Sakura, ready to fight.

The ninja bore down on both of them, aiming his sharp claws right at Sasuke's face.

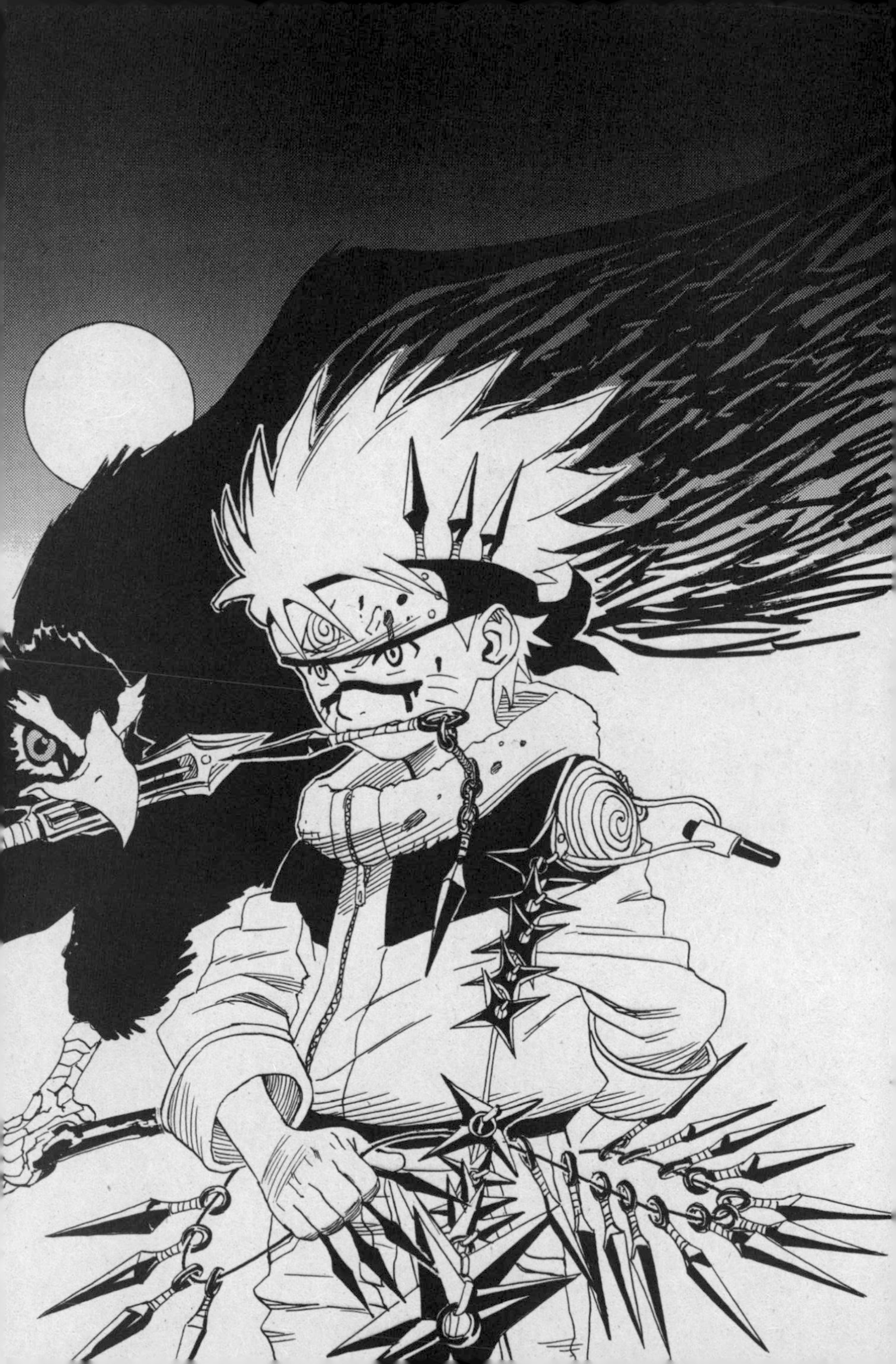

4

POW! **SOMEONE CAME** from the side, slamming the ninja with a blow to the head. He hit the ground hard.

Sakura gasped at the sight of their rescuer.

"Master Kakashi!" she cried. "You're alive!"

Kakashi held the limp body of one of the brothers in his right arm. He reached down and picked up the other fallen ninja.

Naruto was sprawled on the ground. He was still too shocked to speak. Everything had happened so fast. He tried to make sense of it all.

It had looked like the two ninja had taken Kakashi down. Naruto looked over at the ground where his teacher had fallen. A broken log littered the ground.

Master Kakashi used the Art of Transformation, Naruto realized. He had fooled the ninja by making the log look like him, while Kakashi hid in the trees. The ninja had attacked the log. Thinking they were safe, they had moved to attack the others.

Then Kakashi had jumped down, saving Naruto and the others just in time. Well, almost in time. Naruto looked down at his left hand. It was bleeding.

"I'm sorry, Naruto, I should have helped

you sooner, before you got hurt," the sensei said. "I didn't think you would freeze up like that."

He turned to Sasuke. "Good job," he said. "You too, Sakura."

I didn't think you would freeze up like that. Kakashi's words rang in Naruto's mind. It was true. But he had no idea why it had happened.

I couldn't do a single thing, he thought. *Sasuke's never even been in battle before. But he acted like it was no big deal. He even saved my life.*

Sasuke walked up next to Naruto. "Are you okay...you big chicken?"

Naruto jumped to his feet. He wasn't going to freeze up now. "Bring it on!" he challenged

Sasuke.

"Naruto, now is not the time to fight," Kakashi told him. "Those metal claws have poison tips. We have to clean your wound right away."

Naruto gritted his teeth, trying to keep from crying. He had to get through this, somehow.

BEFORE KAKASHI could deal with Naruto's hand, he had other things to do. First, he tied the two ninja to a tree, back to back. Then he turned to Tazuna.

"I need to speak with you," he said.

"What about?" Tazuna asked, his voice shaking.

"Our attackers are chunin—journeymen ninja. They are the Oni Brothers from the Mist Village," Kakashi began. "The ninja there will fight to the death, if that is what they are told to do."

Tazuna's wrinkled face turned pale.

Kakashi calmly paced in front of the tree as he spoke. "Obviously, they were waiting for us to come down the road," he said. "The sun is out, and it hasn't rained for days. When I saw the puddle on the ground, I knew we were in danger."

"Then why did you let them attack?" Tazuna asked.

"I wanted to know who their *real* target was," Kakashi said. He glanced over at Tazuna.

"What do you mean by that?" the old man asked.

"I wanted to see if they were after one of us ninja, or after *you*," Kakashi explained. "But of course, that couldn't be true, because you only paid for a C-level mission. If you needed protection from ninja, that would have been an A- or B-level mission."

Tazuna lowered his eyes. Kakashi had found out the truth.

"You may have had your reasons, but it's a bad idea to hold back information when you are asking for help," Kakashi told him. "We were assigned to protect you from robbers, not from trained killers."

"This mission is way too hard for us," Sakura said, panic rising in her voice. "Can't we quit? We should go back to the village so Naruto can get help for his wound."

Kakashi looked thoughtful. "Hmm, what should we do?" he asked. "Should we turn back now, to get Naruto help?"

Any fear Naruto had was pushed aside by anger. They were *not* going to fail this mission because of him.

I hate not fitting in! I should be the strongest member of the squad! I've been training on my own every day. But I **FAILED.**

Naruto stood up. *Nobody will ever have to save my life again*, he promised himself. *Especially not Sasuke. I won't freeze up. I won't get scared.*

He faced the others on steady feet. "I swear, by the pain in my left hand, that I will protect the old man until this mission is done," he said. **"WE ARE NOT TURNING BACK!"**

6

"NARUTO, SETTLE DOWN," Kakashi told him. "You're bleeding too much now."

The jonin knelt down in front of Naruto. He took a bandage from his backpack.

"Show me your hand," Kakashi instructed.

Naruto held out his hand. His teacher looked closely at the wound.

That's strange, the ninja thought. *It's healing already!*

He looked into Naruto's eyes. The boy looked worried. He didn't seem to notice his strange healing powers.

It's the Nine-Tailed Fox Spirit that's trapped inside him, Kakashi knew. When Naruto was just a baby, the Demon Fox had attacked the Leaf Village. The Fourth Lord Hokage had trapped the spirit inside Naruto's body. Naruto had only just learned about the terrible secret inside him. Sakura and Sasuke didn't know the secret at all—just like the other children in the village.

The power of the Demon Fox had shown itself before. Naruto had used it to perform the Shadow Doppelganger Jutsu. He learned the ninja skill from a secret scroll. Only a high-level ninja should be able to perform it. But Naruto had aced it.

And now this healing power...Kakashi

wondered what other powers were hiding inside the young ninja.

He didn't let Naruto see he was worried. Instead, he bandaged the hand.

"Looks like you'll be fine," Kakashi said simply.

Naruto sighed with relief as Tazuna walked up behind them.

"Um, Mr. Sensei, sir," he said. He looked ashamed. "There's something you should know."

Squad Seven listened, curious, as Tazuna told his story.

"You were right," he said, avoiding Kakashi's eyes. "This job is more dangerous than I told your Hokage. There is a real scary man who wants to see me dead."

Naruto gasped. "A real scary man?"

"Who is he?" Kakashi asked.

"You've probably heard of him. He's a billionaire who controls most of the shipping lanes," Tazuna answered. "His name is Gato."

Kakashi raised an eyebrow. "You mean Gato, of Gato Shipping and Transport? They say he's the richest man in the world."

Tazuna nodded. "That's him. Most people think he's a respectable businessman. But he's actually the biggest crook around. He hires ninja to do his dirty work for him. For years they've been bullying the small shipping companies into selling out to him. Soon Gato will own everything."

Tazuna hung his head. He didn't look like a mean old man anymore—he just looked sad and afraid.

"A year ago, he decided to take over the Land of Waves," Tazuna went on. "When we didn't agree to his terms, he sent his ninja after us. Now he controls all the shipping in and out of the island. The only thing he has to fear is my bridge. Once it's done, we won't need to rely on his ships anymore."

"I get it," Sakura said. "You're the builder

of the bridge. If Gato wants to stop the bridge, he has to stop you."

"That means the ninja who attacked us were working for Gato," Sasuke realized.

"What?" Naruto asked. He was still a little confused.

"But I still don't understand," Kakashi said. "If you knew Gato was after you, why didn't you tell us when you asked for our help?"

"The Land of Waves is a poor country," he said matter-of-factly. "Gato keeps all the money for himself. If I had told the truth, your Hokage would have given me a B-level ninja. We can't afford that."

Kakashi's right eye stared at Tazuna. The

jonin clearly wasn't happy.

"If you all turn away from me now, I'm as good as dead," Tazuna said. Then he began to yell crazily. "Oh well! That's not your concern. You won't be there to see my daughter and ten-year-old grandson cry like their hearts are breaking!"

The old man wailed. He pumped his fist in the air. "Oh! And you won't mind if my daughter vows eternal hatred for all the ninja of your village as she lives her life alone. Heck! IT'S NOT YOUR FAULT!"

Kakashi sighed. "Very well. We'll protect you. But once we get you home, you're on your own."

"Oh, thank you!" Tazuna cried. He turned and began to walk down the path.

Nobody saw the pleased smile on his face.

GOTCHA! the old man thought.

In the Land of Waves, a hut made of branches hung in the air deep inside a dark forest. It was held up with ropes tied to the trees. The hut blended in with the forest around it—the perfect secret hideout.

Gato stood in the middle of the hut. The man might have been rich and powerful, but he was not much taller than a child. He wore an expensive black suit and tie. He glared at the ninja in front of him through his tinted eyeglasses.

The ninja lounged on a soft chair. He was shirtless. His striped trousers were tucked into camouflage boots. Matching armbands covered his bare arms. A mask hid the lower half of his face. His headband was tied sideways around his spiky black hair.

"Don't worry, Gato. I will take care of the old man myself," the ninja said.

"Don't worry? Those two Oni Brothers were supposed to take care of this, and they failed! Don't tell me not to worry!" the little man snapped. "And now all chances of a sneak attack are lost. Those ninja protecting Tazuna will be on the lookout for you."

"Remember whom you're talking to," the ninja replied, his voice rising. "I am Momochi Zabuza, the Demon of ninja who hide in the mist!"

Zabuza pulled a huge sword from behind him. He aimed the long, heavy blade right at

Gato's neck.

Gato backed up a little bit. He might be paying Zabuza, but he knew how dangerous the ninja could be. It wouldn't be smart to make him angry.

Zabuza stood up. "Leave it to me," he said.

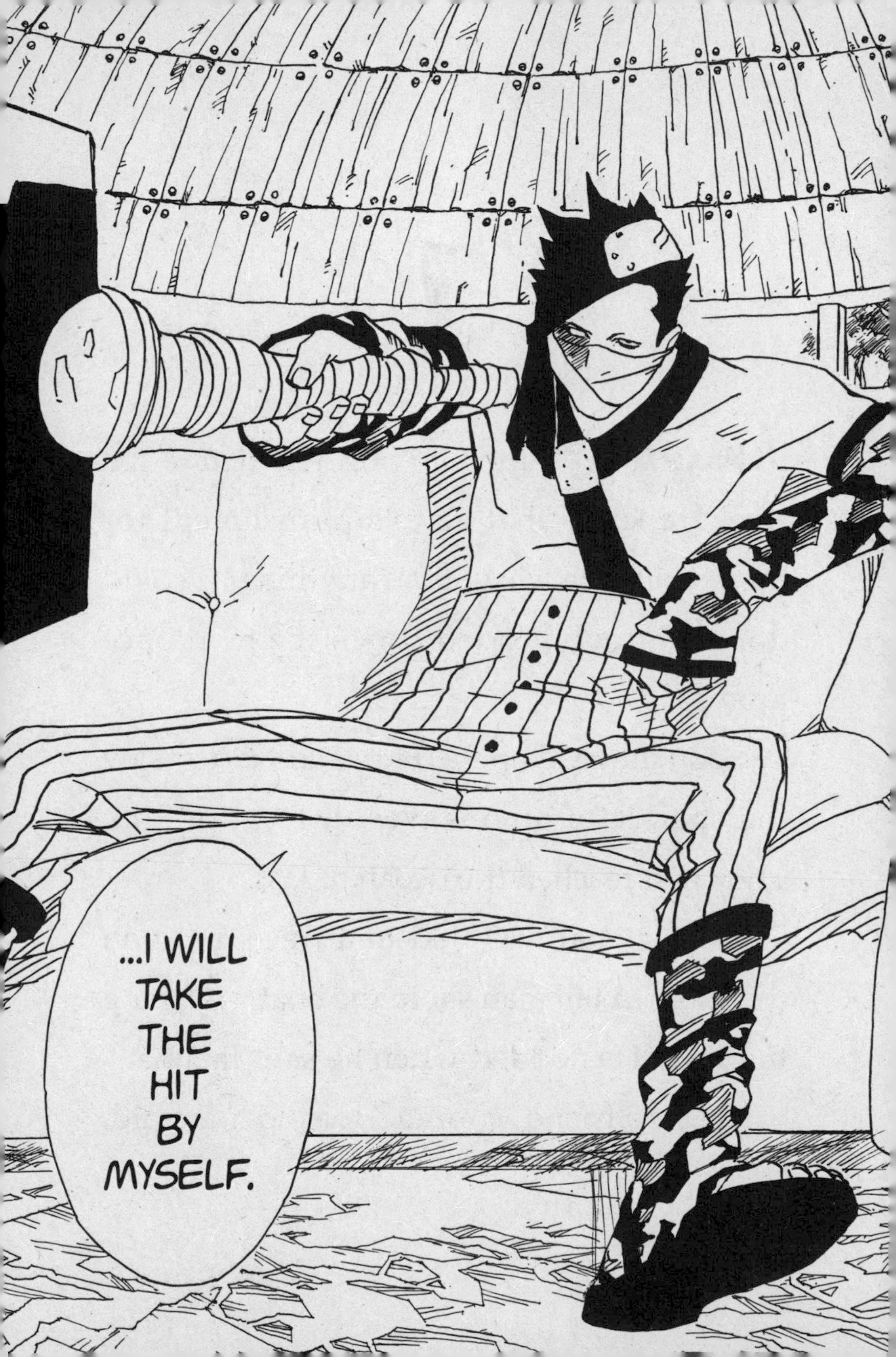
...I WILL TAKE THE HIT BY MYSELF.

7

KAKASHI LEFT the Oni brothers tied to the tree. He knew that Gato's punishment for them would be worse than anything he could do. The group headed down the road once more.

Soon the road opened up, and Naruto saw the sparkle of blue waves in front of him. They had reached the ocean at last.

A long boat was tied to a tree stump on the shore. A tall man sat in the boat, watching the road. He nodded when he saw Tazuna.

"He is a friend of mine," the old man said.

"He will make sure we get to my country safely."

They climbed aboard the boat and Tazuna took a seat in the stern. Naruto, Sasuke, and Sakura sat cross-legged in the bow. Kakashi sat behind them, keeping his eye on the water.

The captain untied the boat, gave it a little push, and jumped in the back. He started the boat's motor. He grabbed a long oar from the floor of the boat and dipped it in the water. As the boat chugged along he used it to steer.

Nobody spoke for a while, and soon the boat steered into a thick fog. The chilly mist made Naruto shiver.

"Wow, this is some fog," Sakura said. "I can barely see a thing."

"We'll be able to see Tazuna's bridge in a minute," the captain told them. "On the other side of it is Nami no Kuni—the Land of Waves."

Naruto fixed his eyes in front of him. Just as the captain said, the bridge appeared through the mist.

"Whoa, it's *HUUUUGE!*" Naruto cried.

Stone pillars rose from the water. They held up a giant stone platform. Naruto could see construction equipment at the edge of the platform. All work on the bridge had stopped.

"Hey, keep it down!" the captain hissed. "This mist will keep us hidden, but from this point on, we have to turn off the motor. We'd be in big trouble if Gato caught us."

He used the oar to push the ship forward quietly through the mist. They traveled along the side of the bridge. There was a row of stone tunnels in front of them. Naruto could see the tops of trees and houses in the distance.

"Tazuna, we've made it this far without being seen," the captain said. "Let's be safe. We'll take an inland waterway into town. I know a pier hidden among the mangrove trees. I can let you out there."

"Thank you," Tazuna replied.

Naruto was curious. Mangrove trees? He kept his eyes straight ahead. He didn't want to miss a thing.

The captain steered the boat into one of the stone tunnels. Naruto strained to see in the dark. What was on the other side?

He had his answer in a moment. A bright ray of sunlight hit his eyes. The boat sailed out of the tunnel into a lagoon filled with

bright blue water. Naruto had never seen such a beautiful color before. And a grove of trees grew right out of the water! Bushy, dark green leaves grew on top of their tangled roots.

"Ohhh...wowww!" Naruto cried out, his

eyes wide.

Those must be the mangrove trees, he guessed. *Trees that grow in water. Cool!*

A pier surrounded the lagoon on all sides. Wooden houses sat on the pier, bleached white from the sunshine.

The captain kept the boat in the shadow of the mangroves. They docked at an empty pier. There were no people in sight, and no sounds except the cry of seabirds overhead.

"This is as far as I go," the captain said, nodding at Tazuna. "Take care of yourself."

"Thank you for taking such a risk," Tazuna told his friend.

They all climbed out of the boat onto the dock. Naruto raced up ahead of the others. He wanted to see everything new there was to see. Sasuke and Sakura walked behind him, and Kakashi and Tazuna took the rear.

"I hope I can make it home in one piece," Tazuna said. He wanted to make sure the jonin felt sorry for him. He needed the squad's protection now more than ever.

"Yeah, yeah," Kakashi mumbled. He didn't want to hear it. He couldn't turn his back on the old man. But this was some mess Tazuna had gotten them into.

They will attack again soon, he knew. *And this time, they won't send more chunin. They'll probably send their best jonin.*

He sighed. Could things get any worse?

THEY WALKED at the edge of the quiet village until they reached another path. This road took them into a dark forest. Naruto tensed up. There could be a ninja lurking behind any tree, ready to attack.

He glanced over at Sasuke.

This is it! Naruto thought. *I'm not going to let him make me look bad again.*

He jogged up ahead and crouched down, listening. If an attacker were waiting for them, Naruto was going to find out. He looked left, then right.

Something moved across the forest floor just ahead. Naruto jumped up.

"Over there!" he cried out in warning. Then he pulled out a throwing star and threw it into the trees. He grinned. The hidden ninja would cry out in pain, and Naruto would be a hero…

But nobody cried out. Sasuke and the others looked at him like he was crazy.

"Uh, guess it was only a mouse," Naruto said sheepishly.

"What mouse!" Sakura shrieked. "Are you

out of your mind? There was nothing there, you moron!"

"Please don't play around with your shuriken," Kakashi warned. "That could be just a teensy bit dangerous."

"Right, don't go scaring us, you little runt!" Tazuna yelled, back to his cranky old self. "Stop messing with our heads!"

"But I know I saw *something*," Naruto said. He ran ahead. Were his eyes playing tricks on him?

He ran out into a clearing. There was a clump of bushes up ahead. The leaves of the bushes moved back and forth.

"Over here!" Naruto cried out. He threw another shuriken.

Sakura reached him first. "I told you to

quit it!" she yelled, smacking him on the back of the head.

"Ow!" Naruto cried. "I swear! There was someone in there!"

Kakashi walked up to the bushes and pushed aside the leaves. A white rabbit hopped out.

"It was just a rabbit?" Tazuna asked. He sounded relieved.

But Kakashi was worried. *That's a snow hare. It changes its fur with the color of the seasons. In winter, when there is very little sun, the fur is white. But it's springtime—the rabbit's fur should be brown.*

The truth suddenly came to him. *That hare is a decoy. Somebody has been keeping it indoors, as a pet. Only a high-level ninja would do that.*

This hare is used so the ninja can create a replacement jutsu.

Kakashi stayed completely still. This was it, he knew. He watched and listened for any sign of their attacker. Then he heard it— a small sound of movement from the trees behind them.

"Everyone take cover!" Kakashi yelled.

Naruto heard a loud **whir** overhead. He felt Kakashi push him down. He landed with a thud on the forest floor.

He looked up to see a huge sword flying

just over their heads. The sword stuck into a tree trunk. Its thick, silver blade was as long as Kakashi was tall. Naruto gasped. He had never seen such a big weapon!

A ninja flew out of the trees, landing perfectly on the blade of the sword. He had his back to them. Kakashi stepped forward.

"Well, if it isn't Zabuza, the kid who ran off and left the Land of Mist," Kakashi said.

Beside Kakashi, Naruto jumped to his feet.

This is my big chance! I'm not going to let Sasuke get all the glory this time!

He started to run forward, but Kakashi held him back.

"Don't interfere," Kakashi said firmly. "This one isn't like the others. He's much more dangerous."

Kakashi sounded calm—almost too calm.

Zabuza glared down at him from his perch in the trees. "You are Kakashi of the Sharingan Eye, I presume? If it wouldn't be too much trouble, could you hand over the old man?"

Kakashi didn't answer. The clearing went quiet as the two ninja stared each other down.

Naruto clenched his fists.

It was time to battle!

Ninja Terms

Hokage
The leader and protector of the Village Hidden in the Leaves. Only the strongest and wisest ninja can achieve this rank.

Jutsu
Jutsu means "arts" or "techniques." Sometimes referred to as *ninjutsu*, which means more specifically the jutsu of a ninja.

Bunshin
Translated as "doppelganger," this is the art of creating multiple versions of yourself.

Sensei
Teacher

Shuriken
A ninja weapon, a throwing star

About the Authors

Author/artist **Masashi Kishimoto** was born in 1974 in rural Okayama Prefecture, Japan. After spending time in art college, he won the Hop Step Award for new manga artists with his manga *Karakuri* (Mechanism). Kishimoto decided to base his next story on traditional Japanese culture. His first version of *Naruto*, drawn in 1997, was a one-shot story about fox spirits; his final version, which debuted in *Weekly Shonen Jump* in 1999, quickly became the most popular ninja manga in Japan. This book is based on that manga.

· · · · · ·

Tracey West is the author of more than 150 books for children and young adults, including the *Pixie Tricks* and *Scream Shop* series. An avid fan of cartoons, comic books, and manga, she has appeared on the New York Times Best Seller List as the author of the Pokémon chapter book adaptations. She currently lives with her family in New York State's Hudson Valley.

The Story of Naruto continues in:
Chapter Book 4
The Secret Plan

Naruto is a boy ninja who's training with his
teammates in Konoha, the Village Hidden in
the Leaves. When Naruto and his new friends
must battle Zabuza, a rogue ninja who is
definitely up to no good, Naruto learns about the
Sharingan, a powerful jutsu that his classmate
Sasuke says Kakashi shouldn't know at all!

COLLECT THEM ALL!
#1 THE BOY NINJA
#2 THE TESTS OF A NINJA
#3 THE WORST JOB
#4 THE SECRET PLAN

COMING SOON!
#5 BRIDGE OF COURAGE